Bold
BOXERS

PLAYFUL! ENERGETIC! KEEN!

SMART! STRONG! LOYAL!

ABDO
Publishing Company

Anders Hanson

Consulting Editor, Diane Craig, M.A./Reading Specialist

Published by ABDO Publishing Company
8000 West 78th Street, Edina, Minnesota 55439.

Copyright © 2009 by Abdo Consulting Group, Inc.
International copyrights reserved in all countries.

Editor: Pam Price
Content Developer: Nancy Tuminelly
Cover and Interior Design and Production:
  Anders Hanson, Mighty Media
Illustrations: Bob Doucet
Photo Credits: Shutterstock

Library of Congress Cataloging-in-Publication Data

Hanson, Anders, 1980-
  Bold boxers / Anders Hanson ; illustrated by Bob Doucet.
    p. cm. -- (Dog daze)
  ISBN 978-1-60453-615-7
  1. Boxer (Dog breed)--Juvenile literature. I. Doucet, Bob, ill.
II. Title.

  SF429.B75H36 2009
  636.73--dc22
                        2008044351

Super SandCastle™ books are created by a team of
professional educators, reading specialists, and content
developers around five essential components—phonemic
awareness, phonics, vocabulary, text comprehension, and
fluency—to assist young readers as they develop reading
skills and strategies and increase their general
knowledge. All books are written, reviewed, and leveled
for guided reading, early reading intervention, and
Accelerated Reader® programs for use in shared, guided,
and independent reading and writing activities to support
a balanced approach to literacy instruction.

CONTENTS

The
BOXER

Boxers are medium-sized **compact** dogs. They have square-shaped heads with short, wide **snouts**. Their coats are short and shiny.

Boxers are smart, playful, and loyal. They are popular family dogs. They are **wary** of strangers and make good guard dogs.

FACIAL FEATURES

Head

Boxers have short, broad **snouts**. They have square-shaped heads.

Teeth and Mouth

A boxer's lower jaw sticks out farther than its upper jaw. It has a powerful bite.

Eyes

Boxers have dark, round eyes. Their eyes are large and full of emotion.

Ears

Boxers have thin, floppy ears. Some owners choose to have them cropped so that they stand up.

4

BODY BASICS

Size

Boxers may grow to be 25 inches (64 cm) tall. They can weigh up to 80 pounds (36 kg).

Build

Boxers have sturdy, **muscular** builds.

Tail

Most boxer owners have the tail shortened. A shortened tail is called a docked tail.

Legs and Feet

Boxers have muscular legs. They are long and straight.

COAT & COLOR

Boxer Fur

Boxers have short, shiny coats. They usually have black markings on their faces called masks. Boxers are either fawn or brindle in color.

The fawn color ranges from light tan to reddish brown. When there are black stripes within the fawn areas, the pattern is called brindle.

White markings are common in both fawn and brindled coats. They usually appear on the chest, face, and feet. Sometimes the white marks are so large that the dog is mostly white. Mostly white boxers are unpopular with many **breeders** and owners.

WHITE FUR

MOSTLY WHITE COAT

Boxers come in many different colors and coats.
The photos on these pages show just a few examples.

FAWN FUR

BRINDLED FUR

HEAVILY BRINDLED FUR

FAWN COAT

BRINDLED COAT

HEAVILY BRINDLED COAT

HEALTH & CARE

Life Span

Most boxers live to be 10 to 12 years old.

Grooming

Boxers have short fur that requires very little care. Unlike most dogs, boxers groom themselves regularly. As a result, they rarely need brushing or bathing. Boxers shed lightly year-round.

VET'S CHECKLIST

- Make sure your boxer gets daily exercise.

- Have your boxer spayed or neutered.

- Visit a vet for regular checkups.

- Ask your vet which foods are right for your boxer.

- Clean your boxer's teeth and ears once a week.

- Avoid exposing your boxer to very hot or very cold temperatures.

EXERCISE & TRAINING

Activity Level

Boxers are high-energy, athletic dogs. They need to exercise outdoors at least once a day. Without lots of activity, they can become bored and **destructive**.

Obedience

Boxers are eager to please. But, they can also be **stubborn** and **mischievous**. Training should focus on rewards instead of punishments. Boxers respond best to fair, **consistent**, strong-willed owners.

A Few Things You'll Need

A **leash** lets your boxer know that you are the boss. With a leash, you can guide your dog where you want it to go. Most cities require that dogs be on leashes when they are outside.

A **collar** is a strap that goes around your boxer's neck. You can attach a leash to the collar to take your dog on walks. You should also attach an **identification tag** with your home address. If your dog ever gets lost, people will know where it lives.

Toys keep your boxer healthy and happy. Boxers like to chase and chew on them.

A **dog bed** will help your pet feel safe and comfortable at night.

ATTITUDE & INTELLIGENCE

Personality

Boxers are good-natured and playful. They adore children and make great family pets. Boxers love to be around people they know. Their courage and alertness make them fine watchdogs.

Intellect

Boxers are clever, independent thinkers. They love to solve problems and show their intelligence.

12

All About Me

Hi! My name is Bear. I'm a boxer. I just wanted to let you know a few things about me. I made some lists below of things I like and dislike. Check them out!

Things I Like

- Being active outdoors
- Playing with my family
- Small children
- Learning new tricks
- Being a watchdog
- Being praised by my family
- Cleaning myself

Things I Dislike

- Being left alone for a long time
- Staying indoors all day
- Strangers
- Harsh punishments
- Other large dogs
- Hot or cold weather

LITTERS & PUPPIES

Litter Size

Female boxers usually give birth to six to eight puppies.

Diet

Newborn pups drink their mother's milk. They can begin to eat soft puppy food when they are about four weeks old.

Growth

Boxer puppies should stay with their mothers until they are eight weeks old. A boxer will be almost full grown when it is 18 months old. But it will continue to grow slowly until it is two.

BUYING A BOXER

Choosing a Breeder

It's best to buy a puppy from a **breeder**, not a pet store. When you visit a dog breeder, ask to see the mother and father of the puppies. Make sure the parents are healthy, friendly, and well behaved.

Picking a Puppy

Choose a puppy that isn't too **aggressive** or too shy. If you crouch down, some of the puppies may want to play with you. One of them might be the right one for you!

16

Is It the Right Dog for You?

Buying a dog is a big decision. You'll want to make sure your new pet suits your lifestyle.

Get out a piece of paper. Draw a line down the middle.

Read the statements listed here. Each time you agree with a statement from the left column, make a mark on the left side of your paper. When you agree with a statement from the right column, make a mark on the right side of your paper.

I like to be outside as much as I can.	☐ ☐	I don't go outside very much.
I want a dog that adores spending time with me.	☐ ☐	I want a dog that is independent.
I like to take control of situations.	☐ ☐	I have a passive personality.
I think short snouts are cute.	☐ ☐	I don't want a dog that snores.
I want a playful, energetic dog.	☐ ☐	I like lazy dogs.
My family could use a watchdog.	☐ ☐	I don't like dogs that bark loudly at strangers.
I am fair and consistent with animals.	☐ ☐	Sometimes I get angry when my pets misbehave.
I want a smart dog.	☐ ☐	I don't like dogs that think for themselves.

If you made more marks on the left side than on the right side, a boxer may be the right dog for you! If you made more marks on the right side of your paper, you might want to consider another breed.

History of the Breed
THE MEDIC'S BOXER

Boxers were first **bred** in Germany during the late 1800s. When Germany became involved in World War I, boxers were trained to perform military tasks. One female boxer, Matthias vom Westen, was trained to find wounded soldiers on the battlefield.

Upon finding a wounded soldier, Matthias would bite off his identification tag. She would bring the tag to a medic and lead him back to the soldier. Matthias rescued so many people that she was awarded a medal!

Tails of Lore
THE BOXING DOG

Laura Comstock was a **vaudeville** star who owned a boxer named Mannie. Like many boxers, Mannie loved to jump. He was so good at jumping that Laura created a short vaudeville act to show his ability.

At the beginning of the show, a punching bag was lowered from the theater's ceiling. When Mannie saw the bag, he jumped several feet into the air and hit it with his **snout**. The bag went flying! When it swung back, Mannie leaped and hit the bag again. Mannie was one dog who really lived up to his boxer name.

FIND THE BOXER

A

B

C

D

Answers: A) boxer (correct) B) Brittany C) Yorkshire terrier D) shih tzu

THE BOXER QUIZ

1. Boxers are good guard dogs. **True or false?**

2. Boxers are not sturdy or muscular. **True or false?**

3. Boxers never have brindled coats. **True or false?**

4. Boxers have long fur that you have to brush often. **True or false?**

5. Boxers are high-energy dogs. **True or false?**

6. Female boxers usually give birth to six to eight puppies. **True or false?**

Answers: 1) true 2) false 3) false 4) false 5) true 6) true

GLOSSARY

breed - 1) a group of animals or plants with common ancestors. 2) to raise animals, such as dogs or cats, that have certain traits. A *breeder* is someone whose job is to breed certain animals or plants.

compact - having a body that is short, solid, and not fat.

consistent - being the same each time.

destructive - causing damage.

mischievous - tending to behave in a way that causes trouble or irritation to others.

muscular - having well-developed muscles.

snout - the projecting nose or jaws of an animal's head.

stubborn - difficult to manage or handle.

vaudeville - a type of entertainment popular in the early 1900s. It featured short acts of comedy, song, and dance.

wary - being careful and watchful about things that might be dangerous.

24

About SUPER SANDCASTLE™

Bigger Books for Emerging Readers
Grades K–4

Created for library, classroom, and at-home use, Super SandCastle™ books support and engage young readers as they develop and build literacy skills and will increase their general knowledge about the world around them. Super SandCastle™ books are part of SandCastle™, the leading preK–3 imprint for emerging and beginning readers. Super SandCastle™ features a larger trim size for more reading fun.

Let Us Know

Super SandCastle™ would like to hear your stories about reading this book. What was your favorite page? Was there something hard that you needed help with? Share the ups and downs of learning to read. We want to hear from you! Send us an e-mail.

sandcastle@abdopublishing.com

Contact us for a complete list of SandCastle™, Super SandCastle™, and other nonfiction and fiction titles from ABDO Publishing Company.

www.abdopublishing.com • 8000 West 78th Street Edina, MN 55439 • 800-800-1312 • 952-831-1632 fax